THE CREEPIEST ANIMALS of THE WORLD

Book for Kids

WONDERFUL WORLD OF ANIMALS BOOK 6

JACK LEWIS

THE CREEPIEST ANIMALS OF THE WORLD BOOK FOR KIDS

Wonderful World of Animals Book 6
Copyright © 2024 by Starry Dreamer Publishing

For information contact:
Starry Dreamer Publishing LLC
1603 Capitol Ave.
Suite 310 A377
Cheyenne, Wyoming 82001
starrydreamerpub@gmail.com

Written by Jack Lewis
Photo Credits: All images contained herein are used under license from Shutterstock.com (See Index for complete list)
Front Cover Photo Credits:
Milan Kuminowsk, Fabio Maffei, Tanya.Asfir/Shutterstock; Creative Commons
Back Cover Photo Credits:
Creative Commons; Ernie Cooper/Shutterstock

ISBN: 978-1-961492-10-3 (Hardcover) 978-1-961492-09-7 (Paperback)
Library of Congress Control Number: 2024916037
10 9 8 7 6 5 4 3 2 1
First Edition: Sep 2024

STARRY DREAMER PUBLISHING

ALLIGATOR SNAPPING TURTLE

Southeastern United States

Hiding in the murky waters of rivers and swamps in the southeastern United States lives one of the most shocking creatures you could ever encounter— the alligator-snapping turtle! Gigantic in size, they can grow to be over 2 feet long and weigh over 200 pounds, making them the heaviest freshwater turtles in the world. These intimidating brutes have an odd red worm-like lure on their tongues that they wiggle around to trick fish into swimming right into their powerful jaws! So sneaky.

3

FANGTOOTH MORAY EEL

Eastern Atlantic Ocean

Freaky Fact:

Fangtooth morays are known to fiercely attack divers and have even been seen cooperatively hunting and coordinating their strikes like a pack of wolves!

Snaking through the crevices of coral reefs is the stuff of nightmares— the fangtooth moray eel! These sinister-looking eels can grow over 5 feet long, with a giant, gaping mouth full of exposed, dagger-like fangs. Their bodies are coated in a thick, slimy mucus that lets them swiftly slither through tight spaces.

Their deadly hunting skills match their horrifying appearance. Fangtooth morays will bury themselves in the sand with their heads protruding, waiting to strike at any unsuspecting fish that swims too close to those menacing jaws.

WHAT MAKES A CRITTER CREEPY?

Researchers have figured out what makes animals seem scary to people. We're most afraid of animals that seem dangerous, disgusting, or uncontrollable. Sliminess, big teeth, venomous bites, sharp beaks, stingers, too many legs, and being active at night with large, wild eyes make animals seem frightening. These features appear threatening or creepy to us. However, just because an animal looks terrifying doesn't mean it's dangerous. Many animals that look scary are harmless and just want to be left alone!

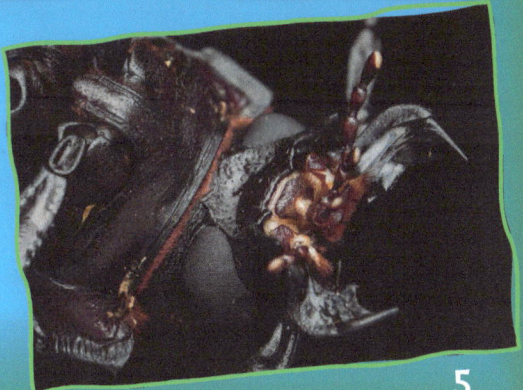

GIANT HUNTSMAN SPIDER
Southern Asia and Australia

Freaky Fact:
Giant huntsman spiders don't use webs to catch food. Instead, they chase down insects with a burst of speed, then jump on their prey and chomp down hard with their strong jaws!

Would you freak out if a spider the size of a dinner plate scuttled across your kitchen floor? Well, you'd better watch out because the giant huntsman spider loves to live in human houses. This colossal spider has a leg span over 12 inches wide! Despite their nightmarish size, they're usually docile and only bite if provoked. These spiders are actually helpful because they eat pests like cockroaches and crickets.

MARABOU STORK

Sub-Saharan Africa

Freaky Fact:
Shockingly, this stork poops all over its legs on purpose to help keep it cool!

With its bald, wrinkled head, long neck, and enormous beak, the Marabou stork looks like some mutant bird! Its naked, scabby head is often stained crimson from feasting on rotting carcasses. From its gaping mouth protrudes a whopping bone-colored bill over a foot long.

Nicknamed the "undertaker bird," this haunting creature resembles a skeleton in a cloak and loves to eat rotting, smelly things. And if that wasn't bad enough, these scary storks have even lashed out and killed children who wandered too close to their nests!

SLOANE'S VIPERFISH

Oceans Worldwide

Freaky Fact:
A viperfish can live up to 30 years!

Sloane's viperfish, also known as Sloane's fangfish, is another fearsome creature from the deep ocean. These fish live deep in the ocean, sometimes as far down as 9,000 feet! They have long, skinny bodies and can grow up to 14 inches long. Their most horrifying feature is their nightmarish mouth filled with sharp, fang-like teeth!

Sloane's viperfish use their glowing bodies to lure in prey. Their big eyes help them see in the dark, and their jaws are hinged so they can eat fish almost as large as themselves!

WRiNKLE-FACED BAT

Central America

Freaky Fact:

This bat's scientific name, Centurio senex, roughly translates to "100-year-old-man!"

The wrinkle-faced bat has a mug only a mother could love! These hair-raising night flyers have wrinkly, folded faces and belong to the bat family known as "leaf-nosed bats." They are found in the dense forests of Central America. Their strong jaws let them eat very hard or unripe fruits when ripe ones aren't available. The wrinkles on their lips help them filter fruit juice and store pulp in their mouths.

DEEP SEA ANGLERFISH

Atlantic and Antarctic Oceans

Freaky Fact:

The male anglerfish is much smaller than the female and will fuse itself permanently to her, living as a parasite for the rest of his life!

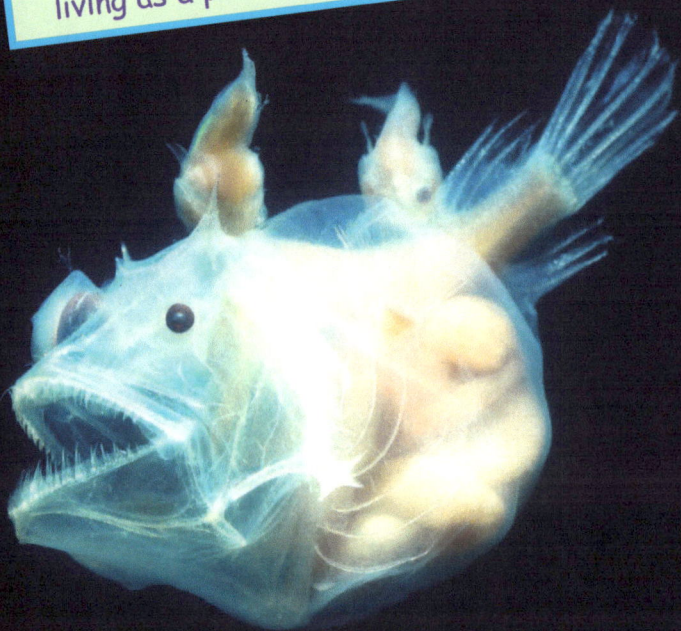

One of nature's most ghastly deep-sea wonders, the anglerfish will haunt your dreams! Lurking in the perpetual darkness over 3,000 feet below the surface, this horrifying creature uses its massive jaws lined with knife-like fangs to ambush prey. These sinister-looking fish can grow over 3 feet long, making them a terrifying sight to behold.

WHY ARE DEEP SEA CREATURES SO CREEPY?

The deep sea is like another world—cold, pitch black, and with crushing water pressure. Animals living there must adapt in strange ways to survive. But these creatures aren't weird; they're perfectly suited for their environment.

In the darkness of the deep sea, color helps animals survive. Many are transparent to stay hidden from predators. Others are bright red, a great camouflage since most deep-sea animals can't see red. Without red light, red creatures look black and invisible to most predators.

Seeing in the dark is important for survival. Some predators have huge eyes to catch tiny bits of light. These big eyes help them find food and mates and avoid danger. Even faint glimmers help them locate food like shrimp and jellyfish.

Deep-sea animals have to eat whatever they can find. Some can expand their stomachs to store food, which digests slowly, so they don't have to hunt often. Others, like the anglerfish, use a bioluminescent lure to attract prey.

We might think these animals look creepy, but to them, we might be the strange ones! Their incredible adaptations are perfect for their extreme world.

TAiLLESS WHiP SCORPiON
Tropical Regions Worldwide

How about this arachnid that looks like a horrifying mix of scorpion, crab, and spider? Despite their menacing pincers and spiky legs, these bone-chilling insects are harmless to humans since they don't have venom or stingers.

At night, they emerge from hiding spots like caves and tree hollows to hunt using two whip-like front legs to sense vibrations. Tailless whip scorpions rely on brute force to overpower prey like insects, lizards and even small birds. Their whopping pincers crush victims before tearing them apart with a set of dreadful jaws.

Freaky Fact:

These arachnids can go without food for over a month!

NORTHERN SHORT-TAILED SHREW

North America

There are almost 400 types of shrews, and most are as harmless as mice. But the northern short-tailed shrew hides a scary secret! This tiny shrew is one of the few mammals that can produce venom. Its potent venom can paralyze animals much bigger than itself. These shrews need to eat a lot—up to three times their body weight every day!

Unlike snakes and spiders, which inject venom with their fangs, shrews use their 32 sharp teeth to bite their victims and drool venom onto them. Ugh!

PACU FiSH
South America

Pacu fish, often called "vegetarian piranhas," have startling human-like teeth and can be found in freshwater rivers and lakes around the world. These disturbing-looking fish can grow up to 31 inches long and weigh up to 55 pounds in the wild. They munch on hard fruits and seeds, unlike piranhas, which eat mostly meat.

Originally from South America, Pacu fish are now also found in the USA, Europe, and Asia. Even though a chomp from them could hurt, they almost never bite humans unless provoked.

WINGLESS BAT FLY

New Zealand

The New Zealand bat fly is a horrifying insect! This tiny fly has no wings or eyes and looks more like a freakish spider missing some legs. It lives on the furry bodies of New Zealand's lesser short-tailed bats. Unlike most biting flies that suck blood, these bat flies eat bat poop! They don't fly or see; instead, they use bristles to feel around and hooks on their legs to cling to the bats. The relationship between these flies and bats is unique. The flies keep the bats clean by eating their droppings, while the bats provide warmth and a safe home.

BASKING SHARK
Oceans Worldwide

Freaky Fact:

It may sound crazy, but basking sharks can leap out of the water like acrobats, even though they can grow over 40 feet long and weigh up to 8,500 pounds!

The gargantuan basking shark with its nearly 4-foot-wide gaping mouth is spooky! These giants swim slowly with their mouths open to filter food from the water. Despite their size, they aren't deadly predators; they just love munching on tiny zooplankton. They often swim near the surface, giving the impression of basking in the sun, but they're really just feeding. These incredible beasts are endangered because of overfishing, boat collisions, and getting caught in fishing nets.

BALD UAKARI

Amazon River Basin

Get ready to meet one of the strangest monkeys in the Amazon rainforest - the bald uakari! These bizarre primates have shaggy orange fur and a hairless, bright red face that looks like it's covered in blood. Yikes!

Their crimson masks aren't just for looks, either. The redness helps the uakaris communicate and even pick mates, with the most brightly colored faces belonging to the healthiest monkeys. So if you see one with a pale, sickly face, you know something's not right!

HELMETED HORNBILL

Indonesia

Found only in the dense rainforests of Indonesia, this shy bird's most odd feature is the ginormous casque, or "helmet," on top of its beak, which is almost solid and makes up over 10% of its body weight. They use their massive casques to joust mid-air with other males, crashing into each other to fight for territory.

These interesting birds are critically endangered due to poaching for their valuable casques and feathers, making them one of the rarest and most mysterious birds in the world.

LOBSTER MOTH CATERPILLAR

Europe and Asia

This bizarro caterpillar starts life looking like an ant to fool predators into thinking it can bite. But then it morphs into a grotesque, bright red form with an alien-like shell, beady black eyes, and a tail that resembles a lobster's fan.

When threatened, lobster moth caterpillars rear up on their back legs and wildly wave their tails like stinging scorpions. If that alarming display doesn't scare predators off, they'll knock them back by firing streams of acid from their lobster-like appendages!

RHINOCEROS COCKROACH

Australia

Freaky Fact:
People will pay up to $100 USD to buy these cockroaches and keep them as pets!

Meet the rhinoceros cockroach - a behemoth bug in Australia that can grow over 3 inches long and weigh more than an ounce! Reported to be the largest cockroach in the world, these subterranean monsters spend most of their lives burrowing underground. When disturbed, they let out a terrible hiss by forcing air through holes in their body.

The next time you hear rustling in the darkness, pray it's not the sound of a jumbo-sized, hissing rhinoceros cockroach scuttling your way.

SAWFISH

Tropical Coastal Waters Worldwide

You might find this prehistoric-looking creature gliding through the shallows of warm coastal waters. This bizarre ray has a long, flat snout lined with sharp teeth protruding like a sawblade.

Sawfish use their menacing saw to stun prey like fish and shrimp by violently thrashing it back and forth. The serrated teeth can also inflict serious injuries when the sawfish defends itself against threats like sharks and crocodiles. Some species can grow over 20 feet long - bigger than a great white shark!

Sawfish are among the most endangered fish in the world due to habitat loss and accidental capture in fishing nets.

Freaky Fact:

Those crazy-looking teeth lining the saw aren't actual teeth. They're modified scales that continuously regrow like fingernails...making the saw an ever-sharpening, built-in weapon.

GiANT FOREST SCORPiON

Southeast Asia

Crawling through Southeast Asia's rainforests, you'll find a scorpion sure to give anyone who meets it the heebie-jeebies! This massive arachnid can grow to be over 9 inches in length and is one of the largest scorpion species on Earth!

Their huge, muscular pincers and thick, segmented tails instantly mark them as serious predators. Giant forest scorpions kill prey like crickets, lizards, and even small snakes by crushing them with their pincers before delivering an agonizing sting with their venomous tails.

FRiLLED SHARK

Atlantic and Pacific Oceans

Dwelling in the inky black depths over 5,000 feet below the surface lurks one of the oceans' most prehistoric-looking creatures - the frilled shark. This living fossil has remained virtually unchanged for 80 million years!

With its grotesque eel-like body, masses of razor-sharp teeth lining its horrible jaws, and a bizarre frilly collar around its head, this shark seems plucked straight out of a nightmare. And those gruesome jaws can quickly unhinge and swallow prey whole!

BUDGETT'S FROG
South America

In the wild plains of South America, the Budgett's frog keeps watch for predators with its big, bulbous eyes. This frog looks like a ginormous mouth with legs, and its entire life revolves around gulping down prey whole. Its bulging eyes are designed for night vision and help it spot victims with ease. When this amphibian attacks, it uses two sharp, tooth-like ridges in its lower jaw to stab and grip its prey before swallowing it alive! Even snakes and other frogs aren't safe from this critter's ghastly gobble.

Freaky Fact:
If a predator comes near, the Budgett's frog puffs up its body, lifts its bottom in the air, and screams loudly like a cat that got its tail stepped on to scare it away!

POTOO

Central and South America

Spooky and a little goofy, these hunters from Central and South America look like feathery goblins with their oversized yellow eyes, gaping mouths, and long protruding beaks.

They're masters of disguise, perching perfectly still on tree branches during the day, blending in so well with their surroundings that they're nearly impossible to spot. And if their peculiar appearance isn't enough, potoos make some of the most spine-tingling, haunting calls in the jungle, which have inspired ghostly legends among the natives.

Freaky Fact:
Even when their huge eyes are closed, potoos have special eyelids that let them still watch for movement around them!

ATLANTIC WOLFFISH

Atlantic Ocean

Deep in the cold, dark waters of the Atlantic Ocean prowls the frightening Atlantic wolffish! These beasts can grow over 6 feet long and have massive heads, with terrible protruding teeth and lips that make them look like underwater wolves.

Wolffish have armored body plates along their sides instead of scales, letting them withstand powerful bites from seals and other predators. Their strange bulging eyes let them scan for prey swimming above.

Freaky Fact:
Wolffish use their immense mouths to crush shellfish, sea urchins, and other hard-shelled creatures with over 300 pounds of bite force!

GHOST SHARK

Australia and New Zealand

Freaky Fact:
Although spooky, ghost sharks are actually not sharks at all!

You'd be forgiven for thinking ghost sharks are make-believe creatures - they look like unearthly spirits gliding through the deep ocean! These ghastly sharks get their haunting name from their pale gray-brown bodies and eerie, dead-looking eyes.

Despite their supernatural appearance, ghost sharks are harmless scavengers that feed on small fish, shrimp, and carrion on the seafloor around 5,000 feet down.

GIANT DESERT CENTIPEDE

Southern United States and Mexico

Freaky Fact:
Giant desert centipedes' special hollow fangs inject venom like a snake!

Meet the giant desert centipede, one of the biggest and most blood-curdling centipedes on the planet. These frightful critters can grow over a foot long and have dark, armored bodies. They slither quickly across the desert floor to hunt for food like mice or other small critters. While their bite can hurt a lot, they usually only attack if they feel threatened.

BROWN COCONUT CRAB

Islands of the Indian and Pacific Oceans

Freaky Fact:

There's a strange but possible theory that the famous missing aviator, Amelia Earhart, may have actually been eaten by brown coconut crabs!

This otherworldly crab is one of nature's strangest curiosities! With a leg span of over 3 feet, it's the largest land-living arthropod on the planet! These monstrous crabs have powerful claws that can lift objects over 60 pounds and even crack open coconut shells with ease. They are intimidating scavengers that will feast on almost anything they can find, including fruits, birds, eggs, and carrion.

HAMADRYAS BABOON

Africa and Arabian Peninsula

Here's a face you'll never forget! These silver-maned baboons live in Africa and spend their nights on rocky cliffs, which makes them look like shadowy figures perched high above. Hamadryas baboons have incredible vision and disturbing, close-set eyes that give them a piercing stare.

BOBBIT WORM

Indo-Pacific Oceans

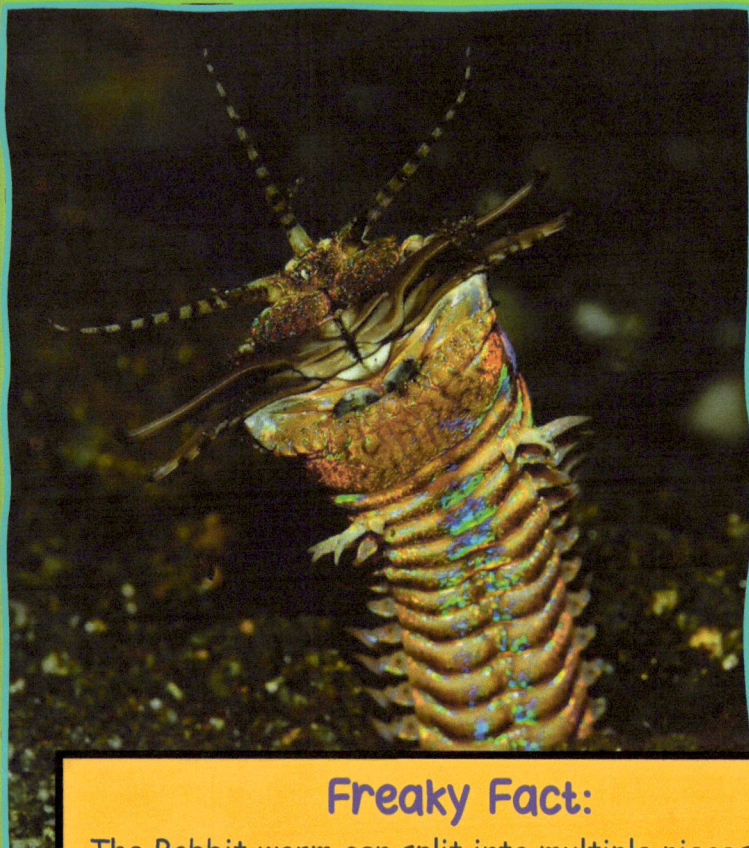

Freaky Fact:

The Bobbit worm can split into multiple pieces, with each piece wriggling around able to live and grow a new head and tail. Creepy!

The Bobbit worm, also known as the sand striker, is a chilling creature lying in wait at the bottom of the seafloor. It can grow up to nearly 10 feet long and has strong scissor-like jaws that can slice its prey in half! They hide in the sand, waiting to ambush unsuspecting fish with a sudden snap of their killer jaws. These deadly worms are nearly blind and rely on their antennae to sense when dinner is nearby.

PIRAHANA
South America

Freaky Fact:

Piranhas are also cannibals and won't hesitate to devour injured or dead members of their own species! Yikes!

Despite their small size, these ferocious Amazonian fish wield a bite powerful enough to chomp through bones and thick animal hide! Piranhas have teeth like razors and are deadly killers when they attack in groups. Usually, they're shy around humans, but when they swarm during a feeding frenzy, they can strip a large animal to the bone in minutes!

TITAN BEETLE

Amazon Rain Forest

The titan beetle is an awe-inspiring creature found in the rainforests of the Amazon. Its intimidating size, which can reach up to 6.5 inches long, makes it one of the biggest insects on the planet! Their humongous jaws, which can easily break a pencil, are used for fighting off rivals and impressing potential mates. Watching these colossal insects taking flight with their powerful wings is a sight you'd never forget!

BAT-EARED FOX
Africa

Freaky Fact:
This fox is shockingly fast and can even escape from speedy predators like cheetahs and hyenas!

If you see a set of gigantic ears poking up through the brush in the grasslands of Africa, you've probably spotted a bat-eared fox! Its enormous ears help this odd fox find its dinner. At night, when most other animals are asleep, the bat-eared fox is busy hunting for insects like beetles and termites to snack on. It uses its incredible ears not just to hear but also to keep cool in the hot African sun. Surviving the dangerous nights of the African savannah, these foxes are masters of the dark!

DEATH'S-HEAD HAWKMOTH

Europe, Africa, and the Middle East

Freaky Fact:

Scientists believe these moths are one of the fastest-flying insects in the world, zipping through the air at 34 miles per hour!

The ominous death's head hawk moth looks like it has a skull "tattooed" on its back and was once thought to bring bad luck! Its favorite food is honey, and it sneaks into beehives by pretending to be a queen bee. With special markings and squeaks that sound like a queen bee, it tricks the worker bees so they leave it alone. Then, it goes straight for the honeycombs, eating as much as it can until it's full!

GOLIATH TIGERFISH
Congo River Basin

If you ever go swimming in the Congo River, you'd better watch out for this savage fish! The Goliath tigerfish can grow over 5 feet long and weigh more than 100 pounds! Its colossal, armored head is packed with 32 enormous teeth that can reach up to 7 inches long - comparable in size to sharks' teeth!

The Goliath tigerfish's iron jaws can easily crunch through prey like turtles and crocodiles. These fearsome fish have even been reported to leap out of the water and kill humans!

GREATER ADJUTANT

Southern Asia

Resembling its close relative, the marabou stork, this ghastly bird stands up to 5 feet tall with a wingspan over 8 feet across. These grim scavengers stalk open landfills and dumpsites in India and Southeast Asia. They use their huge beaks like blades to rip into rotting carcasses and slice open garbage bags. The adjutant's wide gullet lets it swallow whole rabbits, snakes, and other decaying animals in a single gulp!

CAMEL SPIDER
Middle East

Although related, these freaky-looking arachnids are not really spiders! With impressive speed, they can scurry across the desert at up to 10 miles an hour to hunt their next meal. They have special appendages to sense prey like lizards, birds, and rodents, then use their jaws to grind their victim while digestive juices liquefy the animal before slurping it up. While not venomous, their powerful bite is painful; you do not want to get too close!

SARCASTIC FRINGEHEAD

Pacific Coasts

One of the angriest little fish in the Pacific coast waters is the sarcastic fringehead. This grouchy creature gets its name from its aggressive behavior and frightful, frowning mouth that can open wider than its entire head!

Sarcastic fringeheads fiercely defend their homes in ocean-floor burrows and crevices. When threatened, they perform an alarming "gape" display, flaring their huge jaws to expose two menacing rows of sharp teeth to scare off rivals and predators.

Freaky Fact:
Male fringeheads have fierce mouth-to-mouth wrestling matches to claim the best burrows. The bigger the mouth, the stronger the fish!

GiANT WETA

New Zealand

These massive New Zealand monster bugs can weigh more than a mouse and stretch over 4 inches long.

Their name means "god of ugly things," not very nice! They breathe through holes all over their spiky exoskeleton, and weirder still, their ears are on their knees!

Giant wetas were once thought to be extinct, but these ancient creepy crawlers are still around and have been since before the dinosaurs.

BLUE-TONGUED SKiNK

Australia, New Guinea, and Indonesia

The Blue-Tongued Skink is an unforgettable lizard with a shocking blue tongue. These reptiles, found in Australia, New Guinea, and Indonesia, use their bright blue tongues to scare predators and communicate with other skinks.

They are odd homebodies, loving to hide in deep spider burrows, even kicking out tarantulas and wolf spiders to make space. If they can't find their burrow, they might share one with other skinks, which is unusual for lizards.

SNAKE-NECKED TURTLE

Australia

Traveling along Australia's Great Ocean Road, you might spot the freaky-looking snake-necked turtle. Also known as "Stinkers," these turtles unleash a horribly stinky liquid like a skunk if they feel threatened. Their foul spray can reach over 3 feet, so you better stay clear if you ever find one! They live in rivers, creeks, and freshwater ponds, but unfortunately, their habitats are shrinking because of pollution.

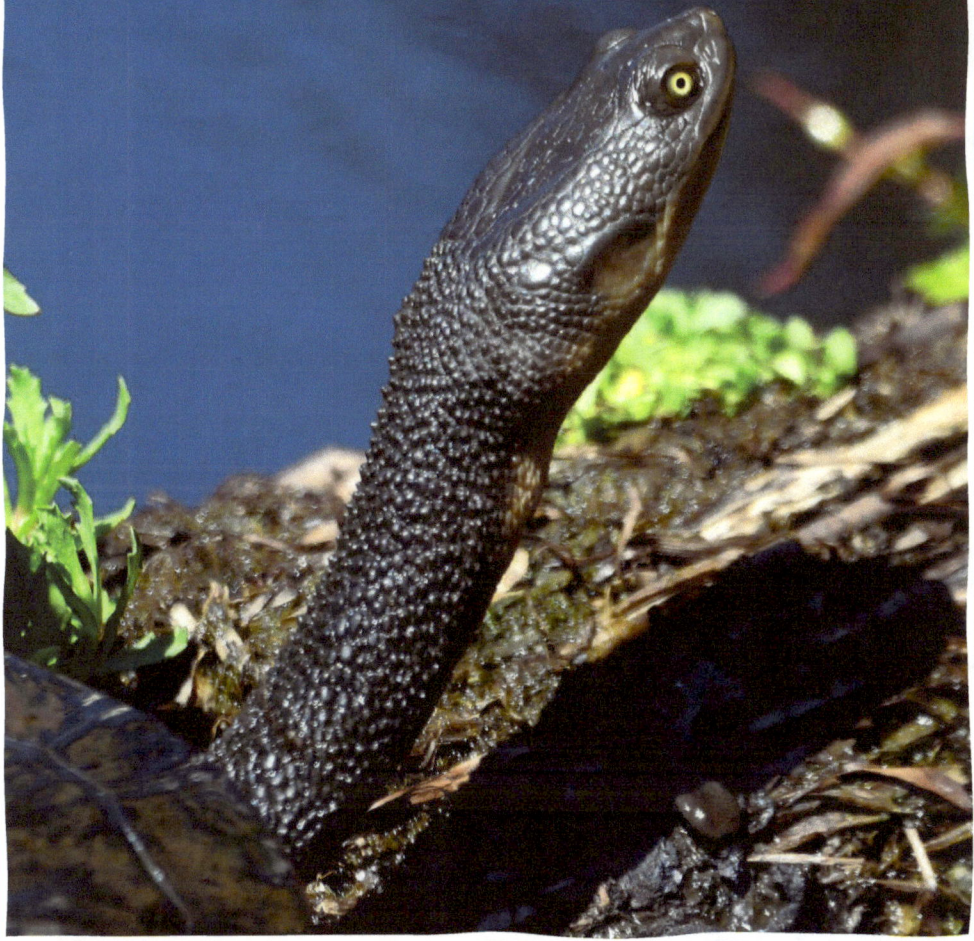

HAMMER-HEADED BAT

Central Africa

In the heart of the African rainforests, an otherworldly creature known as the hammer-headed bat takes flight at night. As its name suggests, this astonishing bat has a head shaped like an immense squared-off hammer.

But this bat's freakish looks are nothing compared to the insane sounds it makes. During mating season, up to 150 males will gather and unleash deafening "honks" and "buzzes" from their massively enlarged throat pouches. It's like a weird bat heavy metal concert!

DEMENTOR WASP
Southeast Asia

Freaky Fact:

A dementor wasp will feed on a cockroach's non-vital organs first to keep them alive and fresh for as long as possible. Yuck!

First discovered in Thailand in 2007, the dementor wasp is one terrifying insect! Named after the soul-sucking monsters in the Harry Potter novels, these wasps turn cockroaches into zombie slaves. After injecting them with a mind-controlling neurotoxin, the wasps then lead the drunken-like zombie roaches back to their nest to be food for later.

51

GOBLIN SHARK

Oceans Worldwide

Cruising in the perpetual blackness over half a mile below the surface swims a ghoulish creature straight from a monster movie - the goblin shark. This deep-sea horror has one of the most unsettling appearances of any shark species.

Its shovel-like elongated snout conceals a mind-boggling set of protruding jaws lined with countless razor-sharp teeth. They use those dreadful-looking jaws to gobble fish, squid and other small sharks for a meal.

Freaky Fact:

Their terrifying mouths let goblin sharks stretch out and extend their jaws super far to snatch up prey. (Look up a video online, it's crazy!)

FLYING FOX

Southeast Asia and Australia

Imagine beasts the size of beagles soaring through the night sky! That's exactly what flying foxes are - some of the largest bats on the planet. With wingspans stretching up to 6 feet across, these fearsome mammals look like furry gremlins taking to the air.

Despite their disturbing appearance, flying foxes are critical members of their ecosystems. They are important pollinators and seed dispersers for many trees and plants. Without them, rainforests would struggle.

Freaky Fact:
Believe it or not, flying foxes are skilled swimmers!

PIG-NOSED FROG

India

Also known as the purple frog, this amphibian resembles a grumpy-looking blob with a pig-like pointy nose! They spend nearly their entire lives underground, only surfacing to breed when monsoon season arrives. That's when the males let out bizarre clucking calls from their burrows to attract mates. After mating in streams, the female hides her eggs under rocks where the tadpoles hatch with sucker mouths to cling to algae-covered rocks.

Sadly, the endangered purple frogs are threatened by humans taking over their jungle homes in India and even eating the tadpoles.

Freaky Fact:

The unique mating calls of the male frogs are said to sound like chickens clucking!

NEEDLEFISH
Tropical Waters Worldwide

Needlefish are silvery, slender fish with needle-like jaws full of sharp teeth. They can jump out of the water at speeds up to 38 mph. Sometimes, they even leap over boats, and their sharp jaws can pierce and injure or even kill people.

These ominous fish are drawn to bright lights at night and can be found near shores and bays. Needlefish don't have stomachs and instead rely on a special enzyme to digest their food. Adding to their weirdness, their bones and flesh are often green or blue!

VAMPIRE BAT

Central and South America

The vampire bat is a spooky creature that lives up to its eerie name! These bats are found in Latin America and are the only mammals that feed on blood. With teeth like needles, they bite into the skin of other animals like cows or horses and lap up the blood that oozes out. One of the most amazing facts about vampire bats is that they can find their prey by detecting the breath their victims exhale from miles away! While their diet is undoubtedly gross, vampire bats play an important role in their ecosystems and aren't considered dangerous to humans - unless you have an open wound.

Freaky Fact:
Vampire bat mothers will sometimes regurgitate blood to feed their young, like a real-life vampire family!

GOLIATH BIRDEATER

South America

The Goliath birdeater is the world's biggest spider! They creep and crawl in rainforest burrows in South America and come out at night to hunt. Despite its gruesome name, this enormous tarantula prefers insects, frogs, or lizards for dinner. It uses its monstrous fangs as toothpicks after it eats its meal. If threatened, they rear up on their hind legs and hiss loudly enough to hear 15 feet away!

BiRD-DUNG CRAB SPiDER

Eastern Asia

Freaky Fact:

Even though predators avoid the spider, flies and other bugs are attracted to the stench and mistake the "poop" for food...only to become the spider's next meal!

This spider is a total trickster - it actually disguises itself as bird poop! The bird-dung crab spider uses its glossy, lumpy body and legs to look like a fresh dropping. The tiny imposter will even add splashes of silk to mimic that wet, splattered look. And if that's not gross enough, it gives off a foul smell like the real thing!

Why such a disgusting disguise? By mimicking bird droppings, the spider becomes invisible to sharp-eyed bird predators who want no part of eating poop.

INDEX

All other images courtesy of Creative
Commons licensing

Enjoy these other great books in the Wonderful World of Animals Series by JACK LEWIS:

The Cutest Animals of the World Book for Kids

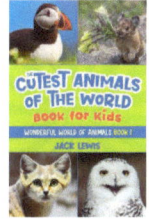

The Weirdest Animals of the World Book for Kids

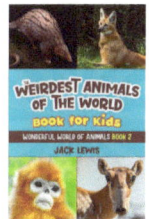

Dangerous Animals of the World Book for Kids

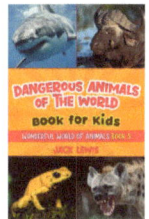

Funny Animals of the World Joke Book for Kids

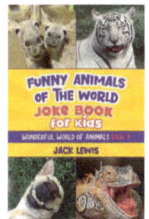

The Grossest Animal Facts Ever Book for Kids

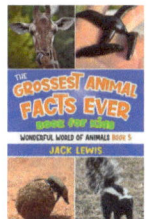

www.ingramcontent.com/pod-product-compliance
Lightning Source LLC
Chambersburg PA
CBHW040937030426
42335CB00001B/24